I wish I had a pet.

Maggie Rudy

BEACH LANE BOOKS   NEW YORK   LONDON   TORONTO   SYDNEY   NEW DELHI

To Laura Ewig Garnier, Patron Saint of Mouseland

JAN 0 2 2015

BEACH LANE BOOKS
An imprint of Simon & Schuster Children's Publishing Division
1230 Avenue of the Americas, New York, New York 10020
Copyright © 2014 by Maggie Rudy
BEACH LANE BOOKS is a trademark of Simon & Schuster, Inc.
For information about special discounts for bulk purchases, please contact Simon &
Schuster Special Sales at 1-866-506-1949 or business@simonandschuster.com.
The Simon & Schuster Speakers Bureau can bring authors to your live event. For more
information or to book an event, contact the Simon & Schuster Speakers Bureau at
1-866-248-3049 or visit our website at www.simonspeakers.com.
Book design by Ann Bobco
The text for this book is set in Old Claude LP Std.
The illustrations for this book are digital photographs of scenes composed of found
objects in combination with handmade elements.
Manufactured in China
0414 SCP
First Edition
10 9 8 7 6 5 4 3 2 1
Library of Congress Cataloging-in-Publication Data
Rudy, Maggie.
I wish I had a pet / by Maggie Rudy.—First edition.
p. cm.
ISBN 978-1-4424-5332-6 (hardcover)
ISBN 978-1-4424-5333-3 (eBook)
1. Pets—Juvenile literature. I. Title.
SF426.5.R83 2014
636.088'7—dc23
2013019359

Do you wish sometimes . . .

that *you* had a pet?

There are so many animals that make nice pets!

But before you take one home,
here are a few things to think about.

Pick a pet that suits your style.

One that is not too big for you to manage.

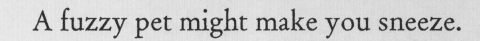

A fuzzy pet might make you sneeze.

A fierce one might scare the baby!

A pet is not a doll.
It might not like to play dress-up.

But it might like to play fetch!

Pick a pet that's fun to care for.

Keep it clean.

Keep
it
comfy.

Keep it fed and watered too.

And when your pet makes a mess, clean up after it.

Every time.

Pick a pet you'll like to exercise.

Because a bored pet . . .

can be *very* naughty!

And remember that some pets
just don't enjoy playdates.

But what about a buggy ride?

You can even teach
your pet tricks—

if you are *extremely* patient.

Most of all, pick a pet
who will be your friend.

Together you'll have exciting times,

quiet times,

and silly times too!

So do you *still* wish you had a pet?

Well, guess what?
Somewhere out there is a pet . . .

who is wishing for *you*!